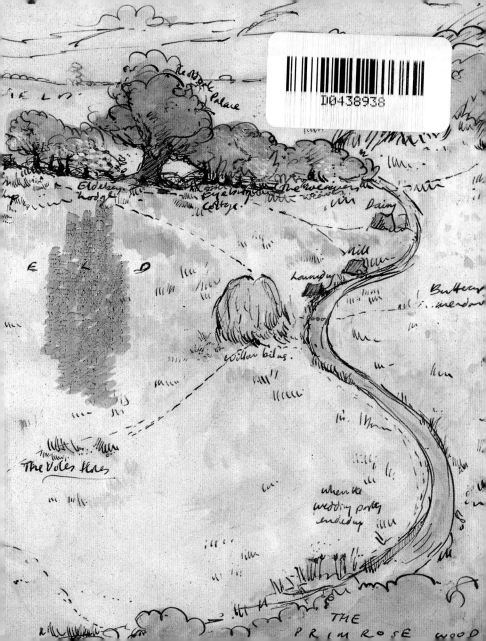

FIELD

FIELD

The Mole Palace

Eldersey hodge

Eyebright Cottage

The weavers

Dairy

Mill

Laundry

Buttercup meadow

willow bitus

The Voles Hles

when the wedding party ended up

THE PRIMROSE WOOD

SUMMER STORY

Jill Barklem

HarperCollins *Children's Books*

For David

For more information visit the Brambly Hedge website at:
www.bramblyhedge.com

First published in Great Britain by
HarperCollins Publishers Ltd in 1980
New edition published 1995
This edition published by HarperCollins Children's Books in 2011

12

ISBN: 978-0-00-183923-6

HarperCollins Children's Books is a division of HarperCollins Publishers Ltd.

Text and illustrations copyright © Jill Barklem 1980

Visit our website at: www.harpercollins.co.uk

Printed in China

BRAMBLY HEDGE

For many generations, families of mice have made
their homes in the roots and trunks
of the trees of Brambly Hedge,
a dense and tangled hedgerow
that borders the field on the
other side of the stream.

The Brambly Hedge mice lead
busy lives. During the fine weather,
they collect flowers, fruits, berries and nuts from the
Hedge and surrounding fields, and prepare
delicious jams, pickles and preserves that
are kept safely in the Store Stump for
the winter months ahead.

Although the mice work hard, they make
time for fun too. All through the year, they
mark the seasons with feasts and festivities and, whether
it be a little mouse's birthday, an eagerly awaited wedding
or the first day of spring, the mice
welcome the opportunity
to meet and celebrate.

It was a very hot summer.

Each day the sun rose high in the blue sky, and the fields shimmered in the heat.

The hedgerow was quiet. Many of the mice preferred to stay inside their shady cottages, trying to keep cool.

Out of doors, the best place to be was down by the stream. The mice gathered there in the afternoon, sat under the bank in the shade, and dangled their paws and tails in the clear water.

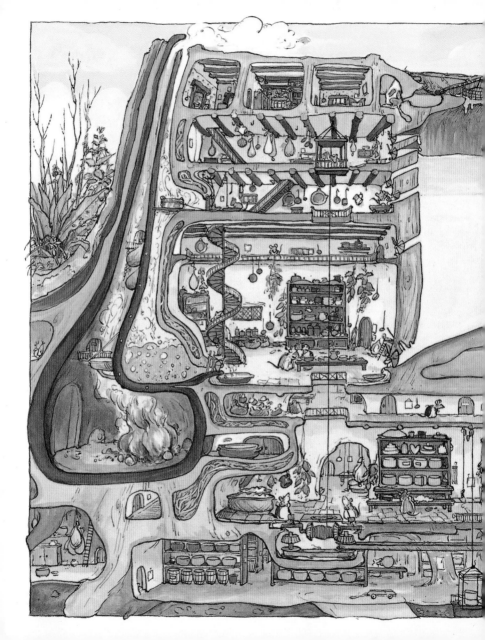

On the banks of the stream were the flour and
dairy mills. The flow of the water turned the
wheels which ground the flour and churned
the butter for Brambly Hedge.

Poppy Eyebright looked after the Dairy Stump.
She supervised the large vat into which milk,
kindly given by some friendly cows, was poured
and stored. The many kitchens, where cheeses
were drained and shaped, smoked and wrapped,
were also in her care.

Poppy was not fond of hot weather. Her pats of butter began to melt unless they were wrapped in cool dock leaves, and the pots of cream had to be hung in the millpool to keep them fresh.

When her work was finished she would wander out by the millwheel, enjoying the splashes of cool water.

The flour mill, further down the stream, was run by the miller, Dusty Dogwood. Dogwood was his family name, but he was called Dusty because he was always covered from tail to whiskers with flour dust.

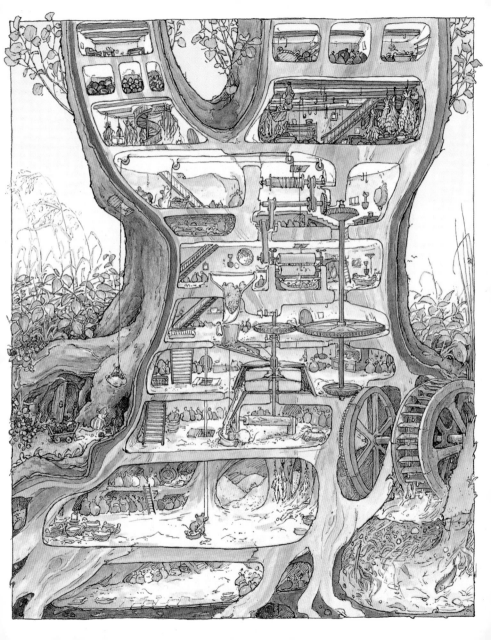

He was a cheerful and friendly mouse,
like his father, his grandfather, and his great-
grandfather, who had all run the mill before him.
He loved the fine weather and strolled up and
down the stream, chatting to the paddlers and
dabblers.

His walks took him past the Dairy, where
he would often see Poppy standing by the stream,
looking very pretty. As the long, hot days went by,
Dusty used to spend more and more time
walking up to the Dairy, and Poppy used to go
out more and more often to the mossy shadows
of the millwheel…

Early in June, Miss Poppy Eyebright and Mr Dusty Dogwood officially announced their engagement. Everyone along the hedgerow was delighted.

Midsummer's Day was picked for the wedding and preparations were started at once. Poppy was so sure the weather would hold that they decided that the wedding should take place on the stream. It was the coolest place, and besides, it was very romantic.

Dusty found a large, flat piece of bark up in the woods, which a party of mice carried down to the water's edge. It was floated, with some difficulty, just under the mill weir, and tethered in midstream by plaited rush and nettle ropes.

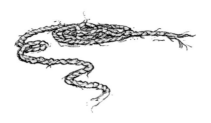

Poppy prepared her trousseau. Every afternoon,
she sat in the shade of some tall kingcups
embroidering her wedding dress, which she hid
as soon as she saw anyone coming along the path.

The wedding day dawned at last. The sky was clear and blue and it was hotter than ever. The kitchens of Brambly Hedge were full of activity. Cool summer foods were being made. There was cold watercress soup, fresh dandelion salad, honey creams, syllabubs and meringues.

The young mice had been up
early to gather huge baskets of
wild strawberries.

Basil selected some white wines, primrose,
meadowsweet and elderflower, and hung them to
cool in the rushes. Basil was in charge of all the
cellars under the Store Stump. He was a stout,
good-natured mouse, with long white whiskers
and a sensitive nose for fine wine.

In her rooms above the Dairy, Poppy dressed carefully. She polished her whiskers and dabbed rosewater behind her ears. Her straw bonnet, which Lady Woodmouse had trimmed with flowers, hung from the bedpost, and her bridal posy lay waiting on the windowsill. She peeped at her reflection in the shiny wardrobe door, took a deep breath, and ran downstairs to join her bridesmaids.

Dusty kept his best suit in a basket under the stairs to protect it from the moths. He put it on and tucked a daisy in his buttonhole.

"I'd better just check that barley I ground yesterday," he said to himself. He ran up the steps at such a pace that the whole mill seemed to shake. The wooden floor above him let down a cloud of dust, all over his new wedding suit.

"Bother it!" he said, sitting on a sack of corn and looking at his mottled jacket in dismay.

There was a thumping on the door below and his friend Conker called through the letterbox, "Dusty, are you ready? It's nearly time to go."

Dusty sighed and went morosely down the stairs.

As soon as Conker saw him, he began to giggle.

"Dusty by name, dusty by nature," he said, trying to remedy matters with his clean handkerchief.

The floury dust swirled and settled again on whiskers, tails, best clothes and buttonholes. The two mice looked at each other and started to laugh. They laughed so much that they had to sit down on a flour bag to recover.

The wedding was to take place at midday and Dusty and Conker arrived just in time. The guests were all in their finest clothes. Three young mice, dressed in smart blue suits, had been chosen as pages and were busily directing everyone to their places. Mrs Apple discreetly tried to dust down the groom and best man, but to little avail.

At last old Mrs Eyebright, Poppy's grandmother, spotted the bride and her little bridesmaids coming through the grass. The pages squeaked with excitement and got into place. Every head turned to watch the bride as she made her way through the buttercups and stepped on to the decorated raft.

The Old Vole, who had been asked to perform
the ceremony, stood up and said in a kindly voice:
"Poppy Eyebright, do you love Dusty Dogwood
and will you love him and care for him for ever

and ever?" Poppy vowed that she would.

"Dusty Dogwood, do you love Poppy and will you love her and look after her for ever and ever?"

"I will," said Dusty. Mrs Apple blew her nose.

"Then in the name of the flowers and the fields, the stars in the sky, and the streams that flow down to the sea, and the mystery that breathes wonder into all these things, I pronounce you mouse and wife."

All the mice cheered as Dusty kissed his bride, and the bridesmaids threw baskets of petals over the happy couple. Mrs Apple wiped a tear from her eye and the dancing and feasting began.

First they danced, for no one could keep still, jigs, reels and quadrilles.

Mr Apple proposed a toast.

"To the bride and groom! May their tails grow long, and their eyes be bright, and all their squeaks be little ones."

The guests raised their glasses and then they danced again. The dancing was so vigorous that the raft bobbed up and down. Gradually the ropes holding the raft began to wear through.

One by one, the little ropes snapped, until finally the very last one gave way.

They were carried into midstream by the current. The young mice squeaked with alarm at first, but as they seemed to come to no harm, they continued with the feast.

The raft floated gently past fields of buttercups and meadowsweet, and the voles tending the fires in the Pottery came out to wave as the wedding party drifted by.

Eventually, the raft was caught in a leafy clump of rushes and forget-me-nots. The ropes were made fast and the dancing began again.

At last the dusk came, golden and misty over the fields. The blue sky slowly darkened and the mice began to think about getting home. All the food was finished up and the pots and pans hidden in the rushes to be collected the next day.

They walked back through the fields in the evening sun, looking very splendid in their wedding clothes. The Old Vole was taken back to his hole first and the rest of the mice gradually made their way home to bed, exhausted but happy.

And what happened to Poppy and Dusty?
They slipped quietly away to the primrose
woods. The primroses were over, but there, hidden
amongst the long grass and ferns, wild roses and
honeysuckle, was the cottage in which they had
chosen to stay.

It was the perfect place for a honeymoon.

THE FAR WOODS

THE

THE

CHEST NUT WOODS

COR

Crabapple Cottage

THE F

Blackberry Pond

Brambly Hedge

Rabbit holes.

N